MARVEL
AVENGERS
MECH STRIKE

THIS IS AVENGERS MECH STRIKE

Adapted by **JEREMY WHITLEY**

Illustrated by **STEVE KURTH, ANDREA GREPPI, AND MARIA CLAUDIA DIGENOVA**

Based on the Marvel comic book **AVENGERS MECH STRIKE**

MARVEL
Los Angeles
New York

All rights reserved. Published by Marvel Press, an imprint of Buena Vista Books, Inc. No part of this book may be reproduced or transmitted in any form or by any means, electronic or mechanical, including photocopying, recording, or by any information storage and retrieval system, without written permission from the publisher. For information address Marvel Press, 77 West 66th Street, New York, New York, 10023.

Printed in the United States of America

First Edition, October 2021 10 9 8 7 6 5 4 3 2 1

Library of Congress Control Number: 2021936333

FAC-029261-21253

ISBN: 978-1-368-07573-2

The city is under attack!
The Biomechanoid is here.

The Avengers come to help.
The Avengers are Super Heroes!

Captain America is the leader.
He fights with his shield.

Thor is the God of Thunder.
He fights with his hammer.

Captain Marvel
has many powers.
She fights with energy.

Hulk smashes the villain.
But it is too strong.

Spider-Man shoots
webs at the villain.
But it is not enough.

Black Widow is fast and smart.
She and Spider-Man
work together.

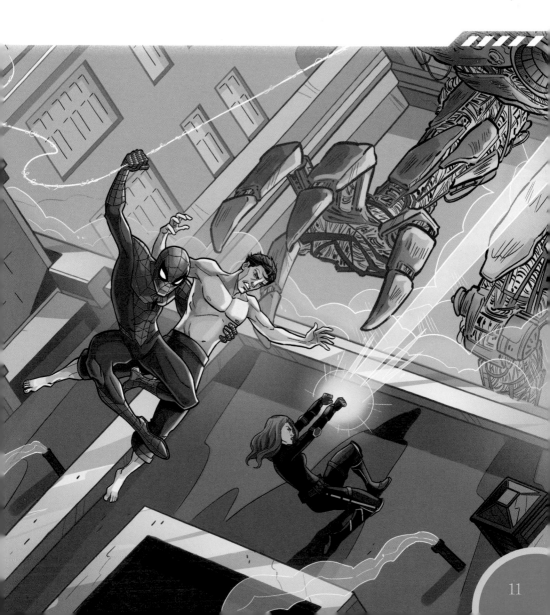

Black Panther has a plan.
His suit is made of Vibranium.
It will make the villain sick.

He jumps into its mouth.

It starts to shake.

The plan works!

More villains will come.
Iron Man and Black Panther
have a plan.

Each Avenger gets a
mech suit.

The suits are made of Vibranium.
The suits will help
defeat the villains.

Every mech has special powers.
Spider-Man's mech is fast.
It can shoot cables.

Captain America's mech has
a big shield.

Thor's mech has a hammer.
It can shoot lightning.

Black Widow's mech has a scan.
It can track villains.

Captain Marvel's mech
shoots energy.
It can fly like her.

Hulk's mech powers up.
It can smash.

Iron Man's mech is
big and strong.
It can blast rockets.

Black Panther's
mech has big claws.
It can leap.

The Avengers save the day.

They will fight again.

But now they need to rest.